The Sleepover Club

CW00745871

Have you been invited to all these sleepovers?

Sleepover Club Vampires

by Fiona Cummings

Collins
An imprint of HarperCollinsPublishers

The Sleepover Club ® is a
registered trademark of HarperCollins*Publishers* Ltd

First published in Great Britain by Collins in 2001
Collins is an imprint of HarperCollins*Publishers* Ltd
77-85 Fulham Palace Road, Hammersmith,
London, W6 8JB

The HarperCollins website address is
www.**fire**and**water**.com

1 3 5 7 9 8 6 4 2

Text copyright © Fiona Cummings 2001

Original series characters, plotlines
and settings © Rose Impey 1997

ISBN 0 00711798 1

The author asserts the moral right to
be identified as the author of the work.

Printed and bound in Great Britain by
Omnia Books Limited, Glasgow

Conditions of Sale
This book is sold subject to the condition
that it shall not, by way of trade or otherwise,
be lent, re-sold, hired out or otherwise circulated
without the publisher's prior consent in any form,
binding or cover other than that in which it is
published and without a similar condition
including this condition being imposed
on the subsequent purchaser.

Sleepover Kit List

1. Sleeping bag
2. Pillow
3. Pyjamas or a nightdress
4. Slippers
5. Toothbrush, toothpaste, soap etc
6. Towel
7. Teddy
8. A creepy story
9. Food for a midnight feast:
   chocolate, crisps, sweets, biscuits.
   In fact anything you like to eat.
10. Torch
11. Hairbrush
12. Hair things like a bobble or hairband,
    if you need them
13. Clean knickers and socks
14. Change of clothes for the next day
15. Sleepover diary and membership card

CHAPTER ONE

Brilliant! It's you! I've been looking everywhere for you. How's it going? Or should I say "Hoots mon! Och aye the noo! And 'Donald where's yer troosers'!" Hey, hey, hey – you're thinking that old Kenny's finally lost it, aren't you? Go on admit it! Well you're wrong, so very wrong. All I'm trying to do is set the scene a bit, you know, get you in the mood for our latest Sleepover adventure.

Whadayamean, it sounds like the weirdest adventure yet if we all end up talking gibberish in a strange accent? That was a *Scottish* accent, dummy, and I am half-Scottish so I should know what I'm talking about.

I know the others wanted to see you first so they could spill the beans. Frankie *always* thinks that she should be the storyteller, just because she fancies herself as a bit of an actress. And Fliss, well, I know that she wanted to tell you about it, because she says that only she can begin to describe how scary it really was. (That's just because she's a big scaredy-cat herself. You should have seen her this time. Talk about quivering mess!) Rosie was pretty carried away by the adventure too, she was so glad that her mum had let her come. But I guess if anyone other than *moi* was going to tell you the story, it should be Lyndz. You see, it's kind of because of her that it happened in the first place.

Now I don't know about you, but I think that autumn half-term is often a major letdown. The weather's usually wet and windy, so you can't spend too much time outdoors. The nights are drawing in so your parents start panicking about you being home early. Summer's so far away you can barely remember it, and Christmas is just a bit of a twinkle in the distance. And basically you're kind of stuck in the middle.

I can't ever remember going away during autumn half-term before, but this year Dad asked us one night over dinner:

" How does a week in Scotland grab you?"

"Ooh I know this one, don't help me!" I piped up. "Is the answer something like 'under your kilt'?"

Mum, Dad, my oldest sister Emma and my yuckiest sister Molly, all stared at me with open mouths. (Molly's was still full of mashed potato so it wasn't a pretty sight!)

"No Kenny," said Dad at last. "This isn't a joke. We've decided that this year we're going to spend a few days with Great Uncle Bob."

I could tell by Mum's face that it was more a case of *Dad* deciding that we were going, there was no *we* about it.

We'd often talked about going to stay with Great Uncle Bob in the past, but Mum had always come up with a million and one reasons why we couldn't. Whenever I asked her what Great Uncle Bob was like, she thought for about half an hour, her face becoming more and more agitated, before finally saying something like, "He's very eccentric," through gritted teeth.

"It'll be great fun!" Dad reassured us, trying his best to ignore Mum's black looks. "We'll be there for Bob's annual party. It's a real treat by all accounts."

"Is it his birthday or something?" Molly asked, all shiny-eyed with enthusiasm (puke!).

"No, it's a tradition he started some years ago," Dad explained. "On the last Saturday in October, he invites everyone from the next village to join him for a massive shindig before winter sets in."

"Cool!" Molly gushed.

My sister's enthusiasm just about made me want to throw up. It's not that I'm a misery guts or anything. In fact there's usually no one who enjoys a good party more than me. It's just that I was kind of worried about someone and I knew that it wouldn't exactly be fiesta-time in their household over half-term.

You're not going to believe it when I tell you that the person I was worried about was Lyndz. Yes Lyndz, our Lyndz, Sleepover Lyndz! I knew you'd be shocked. She's just about the happiest person around, isn't she? Normally. But things weren't normal at Lyndz's place any more. You see, her mum was being a bit – well, weird, basically.

Now you know Lyndz's mum, don't you? Isn't she just about the most laid-back person on the planet? I mean, my mum has always said she doesn't know how Mrs Collins copes with bringing up *five* children. (Yep, Lyndz has *four* brothers, two older than she is and two younger.)

Not only that, but Mrs Collins also works, running a class teaching women how to have babies. She helps out at the local playgroup too. Lyndz's house is always in a mess – part of it is either being pulled down or built up. Mrs Collins just takes it all in her stride and bakes cakes and stuff even though the roof's falling down around her ears. And when we have sleepovers at

Lyndz's, she's really cool because she says she loves having girls around the place.

"You make a nice change from those great smelly sons of mine!" she smiles. And she doesn't bat an eyelid when we get up to some of our silly stunts.

Well that's what Mrs Collins *used* to be like. For the last few weeks she's been really different. She looks kind of grey and tired all the time, she hardly ever laughs and she just seems kind of fed up with everything.

"What's up with your mum?" we asked Lyndz the last time we were over there for a sleepover. "She seems a bit down today."

"Today!" Lyndz snorted. "She's down *every* day. I can't remember her ever being up!"

The rest of us looked at each other and pulled worried faces.

"But your mum always used to be so bubbly," Frankie reminded her. "Maybe something's happened to upset her."

"Well, I think she's kind of upset that we're not going to our grandparents in Holland at half-term," Lyndz confided. "She'd really been looking forward to it, then we had to cancel it. I think it was probably because it was going to cost too much money. I heard her and Dad arguing about it."

"Oh dear!" we all clucked sympathetically.

"But I can't believe she's still upset about that," Lyndz mumbled. "She's known for weeks that we couldn't go."

"Maybe she's really ill," Fliss suggested. "She doesn't look too great, does she?"

"Fliss!" we yelled together, piling on top of her to shut her up.

"Gerroff!" Fliss spluttered. "I was only saying…"

"Well, don't!" Rosie giggled, twanging one of the scrunchies in Fliss's hair and mussing up her beautiful blonde plaits.

"You're going to pay for that!" shrieked Fliss and chased us out of Lyndz's room, down the stairs and through the lounge.

"Chase, chase, chase!" yelled Ben, Lyndz's four-year-old brother, tagging along behind us.

We ran out into the hall – but didn't realise until it was too late that a load of plywood had been stacked against one wall. It was dark so we couldn't see too well, and the first thing we knew about it was when we tripped over it. It came shooting down all over us and all over the floor. It made such a loud CRACK that Ben started to howl from shock.

"WHAT IS GOING ON HERE?" a voice boomed from behind us. "Lyndsey Collins, I thought you had more sense, I really did."

Lyndz's mum appeared with a face as black as thunder. She scooped Ben into her arms and just stood there ranting at us with her hair all over the place.

"I have enough to deal with without extra chaos brought about by you lot. Now you know the rules, Lyndz – stay in your room and don't go chasing about all over the house. Mind you, if your father ever finishes sorting out this hallway it will be a miracle. All my married life I've lived in a mess, and I'm just about sick of it. Now go upstairs and play quietly. I'll call you when supper's ready!"

She stalked back into the kitchen and we slunk up to Lyndz's room.

Nobody said a word until we were safely upstairs. Then we all sank down on Lyndz's bed.

"Crikey Lyndz, I see what you mean!" Frankie gasped.

"Yeah, I mean that sounded more like Fliss's mum than yours!" I agreed. "Has she been taking lessons from her?"

Fliss looked as though she was about to have a go at me. Then she noticed the big fat tears trickling down Lyndz's cheeks.

"Never mind," she soothed, putting an arm around Lyndz's shoulders. "Your mum's probably just having a bit of a bad time at the moment. You know, sometimes stuff seems to get on top of mothers, doesn't it? It'll pass, I'm sure."

We all nodded, although you could tell that really we weren't sure at all.

"Well I hope it's passed before half-term," Lyndz sniffed. "Because it's not going to be a barrel of laughs with Mum like this, is it?"

We all had to agree with that.

And I just couldn't get that thought out of my head as Dad was telling us about Great

Uncle Bob's marvellous party. I just wished there was some way that I could cheer up Lyndz. And her mum.

CHAPTER TWO

When I got to school the next day, Frankie was in the middle of a kickboxing frenzy. I had to dive out of her way pretty sharpish otherwise I'd have had my teeth kicked out.

"Hey Buffy, slow down there! I'm not a vampire that needs slaying, you know!" I grinned, leaping on to her back. We've been best friends forever, me and Frankie. The Sleepover Club kind of came along later. It was at times like this that I felt like we were about four again!

"Ha-*ya*!" She flung me on to the ground.

"How do I know that? Appearances can be deceptive!"

"Well I haven't got pointy teeth for a start…"

"That's a matter of opinion!" grinned Rosie.

"… and blood is definitely *not* my drink of choice!" I continued. "I much prefer Dr Pepper!"

"Aha! You mean you enjoy quaffing a medico's vital juices!" Frankie hovered over me menacingly. "Interesting!"

"Hey Lyndz, Fliss, help me out, would you?" I called over to them. "Buffy here's gone into overdrive!"

But neither Lyndz nor Fliss moved. They carried on leaning against the wall. We could tell just by looking at their faces that something was seriously wrong.

"Wassup?" Frankie, Rosie and I raced over to them.

Lyndz just shook her head and started to sob.

"It's Lyndz's mum," Fliss told us quietly. "She went ballistic again last night, then started to cry and couldn't stop. She said she didn't know why she was so upset, she just felt miserable."

"Is she OK today?" Rosie asked sympathetically.

"She said she was going to go and have a chat with a friend," Fliss continued, not giving Lyndz the chance to reply. "I think that should make her feel better, don't you?"

"Oh yeah!" Frankie nodded. "My gran always says, 'a problem shared is a problem halved'. She'll probably be feeling much better by tonight Lyndz, you'll see."

"I hope so," Lyndz sniffed. She looked so miserable.

We all gave her a big hug, and for the rest of the day we made sure that we did whatever Lyndz wanted. If she was having a rough time at home, the least we could do was cheer her up at school.

I know that as the afternoon wore on, Lyndz started to feel pretty churned up at the thought of going home. But when we saw her mum at the school gates in their big van she smiled and waved at us like she always used to.

"Your mum does look a lot brighter." Fliss gave Lyndz's arm a little squeeze.

"Yeah, she'll be fine now!" Frankie reassured her.

Lyndz gave us a little grin and ran to the van. As we waved her off, Rosie whispered:

"I hope she will be OK. I hate seeing her so down."

I thought about Lyndz all the way home. And spookily, the first thing Mum said to me as I got through the door was:

"Have you got a minute, Laura? I want a word about Lyndz."

"Crikey Mum, how long have you been able to read minds?" I asked her. Although actually that was a pretty silly question – Mum *always* seems to know when I've done something wrong.

Mum ignored me. "Lyndz's mum came to see me today. I think things are getting a bit on top of her at the moment."

I nodded. "I know."

"Well," Mum continued, "I've had a word with your father and he agrees with me. What Patsy needs is a complete rest – away from the house, away from the chores, away from Cuddington."

Now if Dad suggested that, I knew it must be right. Dad's a doctor and he always knows what he's talking about. I'm going to be a doctor just like him when I'm older – after I've finished playing for Leicester City of course!

"Yeah, that sounds like a sensible diagnosis!" I agreed, stroking my chin in a serious doctor-type gesture.

"Well that's good," laughed Mum, "because I was thinking about asking Lyndz's family to come up to Scotland with us for the week. Uncle Bob has plenty of rooms, and according to your dad he just loves having a house full of people. What do you think? I wanted to run it by you first before I phoned Patsy."

"That's a great idea!" I ran over to Mum and gave her one of my Kenny Specials (that's when I hug someone so tightly they go red in the face and start gasping for air!).

"Phew! I'm glad you're so pleased," Mum spluttered, releasing herself from my grip.

"I think it will do them all the world of good. I'll go and phone Patsy now."

As she was dialling the number, she added, "And it means that you'll have a friend there too, seeing as Molly's taking Carli."

"She's WHAT?" I screamed. "Since when?"

"Since last night when she asked me. Is there a problem? Oh, hello there, Patsy…"

A *problem,* she says! Not much! Molly the horrible Monster is bad enough on her own, but when she's with her gruesome best mate Carli it's Nightmare City!

Still, at least if I had Lyndz with me it would be two against two. And I was sure that with all our devious Sleepover tricks we could get the better of them!

Actually, just thinking that made me a bit sad. I wished ALL the Sleepover gang could come up to Scotland with us. I mean, I really really like Lyndz and everything, but it seemed a bit mean going away with just one of my friends. I felt guilty somehow, as though I'd sort of betrayed the others.

"Pull yourself together, McKenzie!" I told myself sternly. "The others won't see it that way. They'll just be glad that Lyndz is going to have a good holiday!"

Boy was I wrong about that!

The next morning when I got to school, Lyndz was as frisky as a new puppy. She was laughing and joking and larking about.

"What's got into you?" Frankie was teasing her as I walked up to them. "Has someone put happy sugar in your Ready Brek or something?"

"Kenny! Kenny! I'm so glad you've arrived!" Lyndz rushed up to me and almost swung me off my feet. "I didn't want to say anything until you were here too."

The others looked at me questioningly.

"Isn't it great?" Lyndz gushed. "Kenny's mum rang last night to see if we'd all like to go up to Scotland with them at half-term. Isn't that brill?"

"Fantastic!"

"Excellent!"

The others all started leaping about too. They were taking the news better than I'd expected.

"Where will we stay?" Rosie wondered.

"What kind of clothes will I have to bring?" Fliss demanded.

Whoa, girls!

"Erm, no, I think you've got it wrong," I mumbled. "Mum asked Lyndz and *her family*."

"Mrs McKenzie told Mum we'd be doing her a favour because she could do with some sensible adult company," Lyndz explained quietly, suddenly aware that she'd just rammed her great size nines into her gob. "But Stuart and Tom aren't coming," she carried on, as if that made the slightest bit of difference. "Mum's sister Lorraine is going to stay at our place to keep an eye on them."

"Kenny?" Frankie stared at me. "Why didn't you tell us about this?"

"I-I-I didn't know until yesterday," I stammered. "I didn't really..."

My voice trailed off as I suddenly saw Lyndz looking very troubled.

"I'm really glad you're coming, Lyndz," I told her truthfully. "We'll have a great time. IT'LL DO YOU GOOD!" I added meaningfully, looking at the others.

The whistle went for the start of school, and I've never been as glad to hear it in my life! I felt bad about the others, but I couldn't help thinking that they were being a bit mean to poor old Lyndz.

During the morning when we had to split up into groups for project work, Fliss, Rosie and Frankie quickly huddled together, leaving Lyndz and me by ourselves. Even Mrs Weaver our teacher raised her eyes at that. And at breaktime, although they hung round with us they kept making catty remarks about how they were going to have the "best sleepover ever" during half-term.

"What a pity you two won't be there to join in!" Fliss told me and Lyndz sarcastically. "But you obviously prefer each other's company nowadays."

By lunchtime Lyndz was a dithering wreck. We were all sitting on a bench when she announced:

"Look, I'm going to tell Mum that we can't come away with you, Kenny. It's my fault that we've all fallen out and I can't bear it!"

Her chin started to tremble and her eyes filled with tears.

"Right then, are you satisfied now?" I turned on the others angrily. "Lyndz needs a holiday more than anyone. It just so happens that it's going to be with me. If there was a way to invite you all up to Scotland I would, believe me. But Great Uncle Bob's about ninety or something. I don't think it would be very good for his health if we *all* descended on him, do you?"

The others shook their heads and looked suitably ashamed. They gave Lyndz an extra big hug.

"Sorry for being so mean," Frankie told her. "You go and have fun – just not *too* much, OK?"

At least we were all friends again, which was the main thing. But my big speech back there had got me thinking. Why couldn't we all go up to Scotland? Uncle Bob wasn't *really* ninety, and Dad had already said that he had loads of rooms and loved having his house full of people. What could be better than having it full of my friends? I knew that

Mum would be speaking to him that night to confirm the arrangements, so I'd have to ask her if the rest of the gang could come with us before she phoned.

All afternoon I rehearsed how I would ask her. The only problem was that as far as Mum was concerned, us Sleepover girls together meant only one thing – TROUBLE. And it was one thing coping with that in your own home, but quite another transporting it hundreds of miles up into the wilds of Scotland.

I decided to just grab the bull by the horns and ask Mum straight out as soon as I got home. But it was just my luck that she was tackling Dad's paperwork. Now if there's one thing I've learnt in my ten years on this planet, it is *never* to disturb Mum when she's got her business-head on. The fall-out can be pretty spectacular – I still have the scars to prove it! And it was the worst luck ever that she had her business-head on all through dinner and all through the rest of the evening. In fact she only snapped out of it when the phone rang.

"Oh Uncle Bob!" she spoke crisply into the receiver. "I was just about to ring you."

Drat, drat and double blooming drat covered in bogies. I was too late – there was no way that the rest of the Sleepover gang could come up to Scotland with us now!

CHAPTER THREE

Whilst Mum chatted to Great Uncle Bob, I sat on the stairs and put my head in my hands. I'd let my chums down big time. I know that they weren't expecting to go to Scotland with us or anything, but I'd kind of got used to the idea in my head.

I'd never been to Great Uncle Bob's house before, but I imagined it was like this enormous castle overlooking a lake. I figured that it would have about fifty bedrooms and they'd all have four-poster beds and jacuzzi baths just like the one Fliss has, only much bigger. I imagined the five of us swimming in the lake. Well, maybe Fliss wouldn't actually swim in the lake, she'd just hover at the edge looking pretty...

"... Laura! Laura! For goodness sake, stop daydreaming! Uncle Bob wants a word with you!" Mum was holding out the receiver to me and looking very impatient.

What on earth could he want with me? I hadn't been listening to Mum's conversation at all, so I didn't know what she'd told him about Lyndz and her family. Maybe he was going to explain to me why they couldn't stay with us after all. I braced myself for the worst.

"Er, h-hello?" I stammered, taking the phone from Mum.

"Kenny! How are you?" a warm chuckly voice asked.

Now any adult who calls me Kenny instead of my stupid proper name is all right by me.

"Fine thanks!" I grinned.

"So I'm finally going to meet you *and* one of your friends – two for the price of one, eh?" he guffawed.

"Erm yes, thanks for letting Lyndz come

too, Great Uncle Bob," I said. "We really appreciate it."

"The more the merrier. How are the rest of your Sleepover chums?" he asked.

Well, you could have knocked me down with a feather! How on earth did he know about *them*?

"Erm, fine thanks," I whispered. I was beginning to see why Mum thought the guy was a bit strange.

"It seems such a pity that only one of your friends is going to accompany you up to Bonny Scotland. How about inviting the others as well? What are their names again? Frankie, Fliss and who's the other one?"

The guy was seriously starting to spook me out now.

"R-Rosie!" I squeaked.

"Ah yes, that's the one!" he chuckled. "I love reading about your sleepover exploits in your Christmas letters!"

Phew! So that's how he knew about the Sleepover gang. (Mum makes us write these stupid letters to our rellies at Crimbo time and I always fill mine with stuff about our best sleepovers and of course news of Leicester City FC!)

Anyway, when I'd recovered myself I suddenly realised what Great Uncle Bob had suggested. It was like he could really read my mind!

"Thanks, Great Uncle Bob!" I screamed. "That'd be brilliant! I'll ask them all tomorrow."

"Oh Kenny – there's just one thing before you go."

"Yes?"

"Do you think you could just call me 'Uncle Bob'? I don't want to feel like a doting old fool just yet!"

I grinned. "OK Uncle Bob, you've got it. See ya!"

I handed the phone over to Dad, who was hovering by my shoulder. This was just *wicked*! I couldn't wait to see the others at school the next day. But I was going to make sure that I had some fun with them first.

The next morning I was in the playground first for once. As soon as Rosie appeared, I started doing this crazy jig.

"You look like a turkey with a firework up its bottom!" she shrieked. "What on earth are you doing?"

"The highland fling!" I shouted, throwing myself into my dancing with gusto. "Lyndz and I have to learn it for Uncle Bob's party. It's going to be wicked."

"Oh!" Rosie's face fell. "Right."

"Yeah, he has this mega big party every year and we're going to be there for it. It's going to be ace! Hey Lyndz, I'm going to have to teach you the highland fling before we go up to Scotland, you know!"

Lyndz was walking into the playground with Frankie and Fliss. She looked kind of embarrassed when I mentioned the Scottish trip, like she didn't want to upset the others or something. But I didn't let that stop me.

"Uncle Bob's got this stonking great pile of a house. It's really mega. You'd love it, guys!" I looked round the others then clapped my hand over my mouth. "Oops sorry, I forgot! Still, Lyndz and I'll tell you all about it when we get back, won't we?"

Lyndz just went bright red and looked at

her feet. The others looked seriously peeved.

But I didn't stop there. By lunchtime I'd told them that Uncle Bob had hundreds of servants, including chefs who could knock up any delicacy you fancied. I'd also told them how all the guests at his party would be in the height of fashion and dripping in diamonds. You should have seen their faces! Honestly, if looks could kill, I'd be dead a million times over.

I was just about to launch into a description of Uncle Bob's (imaginary) helicopter and speedboat when Frankie snarled:

"OK McKenzie, I think we get the picture! You and Lyndz are going to have a fantastic time in Scotland and we're not. Well quite frankly I pity Lyndz. I wouldn't want to spend all my half-term with such a bragger. I don't know what's got into you, Kenny. You're not the same girl we used to know."

The others stared at me hard and shook their heads. Even Lyndz was looking at me sadly.

"We wouldn't come to Scotland with you if you paid us, would we girls?" Frankie growled.

"No way!"

"No thanks!"

I grinned. My plan had worked.

"Well that's a pity," I said innocently. "Because I *was* going to ask you all if you wanted to come with us too!"

"You're kidding!" The others started doing impressions of goldfishes with their mouths open.

"No, straight up," I admitted. "Uncle Bob invited you himself last night. I was just winding you up to pay you back for being so mean yesterday!"

"Kenny, you creep!" Frankie leapt on to my back.

"Still, if you're not going to come it doesn't matter," I shrugged, shaking her off.

"'Course we will, you dill!" Frankie grinned. "Especially if your Uncle's place is as fantastic as you say."

"Ah well, I actually made that up!" I confessed. "I've never even been there myself. It could be one big run-down old shack for all I know."

"Oh well, in that case," Rosie said jokingly,

"I don't think we should go. What do you think, Fliss?"

"Well erm, I don't think Mum would let me go anyway," Fliss admitted sheepishly.

"WHAT?" I almost screamed. "You gave Lyndz and me such a hard time yesterday because you weren't coming with us and now you say you can't come anyway? There's no pleasing some people!"

"Mum needs me to help out with the twins," Fliss told us huffily. "She's always saying how she'd be lost without me."

"But you will ask her, won't you Fliss? It'll be a laugh," Frankie giggled.

Then she turned to me. "Kenny, you are serious about this, aren't you? This isn't another one of your sick jokes?"

"I'm seriously serious," I reassured them. "Just ask your parents tonight and let me know tomorrow."

I felt all kind of warm and happy as we walked home from school. Not only would Lyndz be having a better half-term than she expected – we all would!

I thought the worst thing about the whole

deal would be waiting until the following day to see whether the others could go. But that evening our phone was ringing hot on the hook. And do you know who the first person to ring was? Only Mrs Proudlove, Fliss's mum.

As soon as I heard her voice on the other end I thought, "Oh-oh, trouble." We'd never hear the end of it if Fliss really couldn't go, because as you well know she hates being left out of anything. And her mum does tend to fuss over nothing. I just knew that she would be panicking about how far away Scotland was, and who would be taking care of her precious baby in her absence.

Well, it just goes to show how much *I* know.

"That was Fliss's mum," said Mum as she came off the phone about three hours later. Hell-o Mum, I knew that, I answered the phone, remember?

"She just rang to check arrangements for Scotland and to thank us for taking Fliss with us."

"What?" I asked, stunned. "You mean she can come?"

"She certainly can! Nikki seemed quite relieved to have her off her hands, to be honest with you."

Now that I could believe.

Ten seconds later the phone rang again. It was Frankie.

"I can come, I can come!" she squealed down the phone. "Is your mum around so my mum can discuss the arrangements with her?"

Whilst Mum was still on the phone Molly returned from Carli's.

"Who's that?" She gestured to the phone.

"Frankie's mum. Not that it's any of your business!"

"What did *she* want, then?" Molly demanded as soon as Mum had put the phone down. But I could guess by her aggressive tone that she'd already figured out the answer.

"Uncle Bob asked me to invite the rest of my mates to Scotland with us," I smiled evilly. "I guess he knows that you've only got the one friend to invite!"

Molly made a lunge for me.

"That'll do, you two," said Mum sharply. "If there's going to be any trouble, neither of you will be coming. You can go and stay at Gran's with Emma."

I should explain that Emma our older sister had to study for exams over half-term, so she was staying with our grandparents in Cuddington.

"Well, how are we all going to get up there?" Molly demanded. "There won't be enough room in our car."

Oh no! I hadn't even thought about that! Fortunately Mum had.

"I know that, Molly. That's why Lyndz's parents will be taking all the girls in their van."

Wicked!

The only person we hadn't heard from was Rosie-Posie, and I just knew that there wouldn't be a problem with her. Her mum's always a bit strapped for cash since her dad left, and they never get much of a chance to get away. I knew that she'd be keen to let Rosie have a break with us.

Well, I was wrong again! When I got to school the next morning, the others were all in a huddle in the playground. I figured they'd all be chatting excitedly about Scotland, but they looked dead miserable.

"Whassup?" I rushed over to them.

"Rosie can't come with us," Fliss said quietly.

"No! Why not?"

"It's Mum's new boyfriend Richard, he wants us all to go somewhere together," Rosie sniffed. "I tried to persuade Mum, really I did, but there was no way she was going to budge. She really likes this guy and she said this was really important to her. What could I do?"

Rosie put her hands over her eyes and her shoulders started to shake. Fliss put her arm round her and Lyndz and Frankie looked glumly at their feet.

I felt gutted. It just wouldn't be the same if we weren't all together.

"I don't know what to say Rosie, I really don't," I admitted. "We're just not going to enjoy Scotland so much now, are we guys?"

Nobody said anything. I looked at Frankie – and I swear she was *laughing*! Lyndz was bright red in the face and starting to splutter, and Fliss was trying so hard not to laugh that she was snorting down her nose.

"Guys?"

"FOOLED YOU!" they all yelled together.

"You're not the only one who can wind people up, you know!" giggled Rosie, slapping me on the shoulder.

"You mean you *can* come?" I asked, gobsmacked.

"'Course I can!" Rosie smiled. "Richard had mentioned about going away but when I told him about your Great Uncle Bob's place he said it sounded a lot of fun and I should definitely go. He says we can go away another time. Isn't that cool?"

"Not as cool as us all going away together!" I said, and we all started doing a crazy jig right there in the middle of the playground.

"Well, Uncle Bob, you'd better watch out!" I sang. "'Cos Scotland here we come!"

CHAPTER FOUR

For the next few days, right up until half-term, all we could talk about was Scotland and what a wicked time we were going to have. I swear that even our breath turned tartan.

Fliss's main concern was – surprise, surprise – what clothes she was going to take.

"I've got this cool little mini kilt with a dinky pin, and an Aran sweater – that's Scottish, isn't it? And I saw these great checked cropped trousers in Gap, Mum might buy those for me too."

"Get a life!" I scoffed. "All Mum said was that you should take plenty of warm things and some sturdy walking shoes. So that doesn't mean your silver stilettos, all right Fliss?"

"But what about the party?" asked Rosie. "Surely we'll need something posh for that."

"I doubt it. The villagers who go won't exactly expect to see us wearing tiaras," I reassured her. "Just take whatever's comfortable. I know what I'll be wearing..."

"... Your Leicester City football kit!" chimed in the others. "Yes, we know!"

"Although I do think you ought to make a bit of an effort for your Great Uncle," Fliss told me seriously. "You don't want to let him down, do you?"

How I stopped myself from punching her in the hooter I'll never know. Fliss gets me like that sometimes. And the thing is, she has absolutely no idea at all that she's winding me up. Although she wound *everybody* up on the day we actually set off for Scotland – and everybody made sure she knew about that!

To be fair, it wasn't all Fliss's fault that the start of our holiday was a disaster. My dad had a hand in it too – or at least one of his patients did. Now I know that doctors are there to serve their patients. And I know that saving lives is one of the most important jobs in the whole world. But why did Mrs Fogarty decide that 10.30 on Saturday morning was the ideal time to ring Dad to say that her son was seriously ill? I mean, we were all packed up and ready to go to Lyndz's to meet up with the others.

"Mrs Fogarty, you really ought to call the surgery," Dad told her gently as we all stood around tutting and pointing at our watches. "Of course they'll see a patient if it's an emergency. No Mrs Fogarty, I wouldn't want a death on my conscience, but I am pretty... all right then Mrs Fogarty, I will come round as soon as I can."

"DAD!" Molly and I yelled together.

"Look, her son just might have meningitis and you can't play around with that. I'll be back as soon as I can. You'd better ring Patsy and Keith and explain the situation to them."

And with that, Dad grabbed his doctor's bag and flew out of the door.

Now if I was a doctor, I don't really know what I would have done. But just at that moment I wasn't thinking about being a doctor. I was just thinking about meeting up with my mates and getting up to Scotland to have some fun.

Eleven o'clock passed. And half past. It was almost midday when Dad finally reappeared. I was certain that the boy had had to go to hospital for sure.

"Well?" we asked when Dad finally came through the door. We could tell by the look on his face that it wasn't good news.

"A temperature and a runny nose. The lad has a wee cold," he told us grimly. "I spent half an hour trying to reassure the woman that her son was not on death's door, and then I had to go to the surgery to inform the other doctors. You couldn't make me a cup of tea, could you Molly love? I feel exhausted and I've still got that long drive ahead of me."

Talk about spitting feathers! We'd never get up to Scotland at this rate.

When we did eventually set off, I hadn't been in the car five minutes before I'd had a fight with Molly, called Carli a brainless chicken and been told by Mum that if I carried on I wouldn't be going to Scotland at all. Needless to say, by the time we drew up in front of Lyndz's I was well cheesed off. Not in the best of moods then to cope with Fliss bawling her eyes out and having what looked like a full-on paddy.

"What's with her?" I asked Frankie, who was looking a bit pink round the edges.

"She's just discovered that she's brought her brother Callum's bag instead of her own."

She gestured to the pyjamas covered in Pokémon and Pikachu which were scrunched up on the gravel.

"You ought to have seen her when she found out!" Rosie whispered. "She went ballistic. She flung everything out over the ground and started stamping on them."

"I bet Callum did the same when he found Fliss's frilly knicks in his bag!" I grinned. "Where is he anyway?"

"That's just the point," whispered Frankie. "He's gone to stay with their gran for a few days. But when Lyndz's mum rang Fliss's mum to find out where they were, Fliss's mum didn't know and thought they'd gone off somewhere – with Fliss's bag!"

"Trust Fliss!" I snarled. "It can't be that hard to check that you've got the right bag can it? Even for Fliss."

Was this holiday turning into a disaster or what?

"So what are we doing now?" I demanded. "Waiting for Callum to turn up?"

"No, Fliss's mum is packing her another bag and Andy's going to bring it over," Lyndz explained. "He shouldn't be long because Mum rang him ages ago. I'm really cross with Fliss, actually. Before this happened Mum was quite bright, but she's gone all cross and narky again."

"She's not the only one," I said through gritted teeth.

After what felt like an hour (but was apparently only five minutes) Andy's van appeared. He leapt out brandishing a luggage bag identical to the one whose contents were now being tried on gleefully by Ben and Spike, Lyndz's two youngest brothers.

"Here you are love," he smiled, thrusting it towards Fliss. "We managed to trace your gran and get your bag back. Now, now, there's no need to cry!"

Fliss was in full waterworks mode again and was sobbing into Andy's jumper. Mum managed to prise her away, and before any more mishaps could occur bundled us all into Lyndz's van.

"OK Jim, I've got the directions and your mobile number. You've got mine, haven't you?" Lyndz's dad checked with mine. "Right then, all being well we'll rendez-vous at Tebay service station. All aboard? Wagons roll!"

At last! We were off! I have to admit that at one stage I seriously doubted that we would ever get out of Cuddington.

"Can we have the Steps tape on, Mum?" Lyndz asked.

"Yeah!"

"Wheels On The Bus!" yelled Ben.

"Steps!" we all chorused back.

"Wheels On The Bus!" Ben's chin was going all wobbly.

"OK, you can have your tape on first, Ben," Lyndz caved in. "But then it's our turn, all right?"

Ben grinned his big soppy grin and started doing all the actions to the songs on his tapes. The first time round we all joined in and it was a bit of a laugh. But when Ben insisted on having his tape on again, my heart sank. Not least because the alternative to his stupid tape was him shrieking at the top of his voice.

"Just once more then." Lyndz shrugged her shoulders apologetically at the rest of us.

I wouldn't have cared, but Mrs Collins just didn't say anything at all. So we had to listen to "Wheels On The Stupid Bus" yet again. And let me tell you, by the fifth time I was ready to yank the wheels *off* the nearest bus and stuff them down Ben's throat.

Fortunately, five repeats of his tape seemed more than enough for Ben too, because he nodded off.

"Great!" whispered Rosie. "Can we have Steps on now?"

We handed the tape to Mrs Collins who put it on. Then, noticing that Ben was asleep, she turned the volume right down so we could barely hear it at all.

"Could we have it up just a tiny bit, Mrs Collins?" Fliss asked.

"I don't want to wake up Ben, Felicity," Lyndz's mum replied coldly. "He wouldn't be so tired if we'd managed to get off on time in the first place."

"Patsy!" Mr Collins looked crossly at his wife.

Fliss went bright red and her eyes welled up with tears. Lyndz squeezed her arm and mouthed "sorry". She looked as though she was about to start crying herself. The rest of us just looked miserable. So much for Mum's plan of bringing Lyndz's mum away with us to cheer her up. At the moment she just seemed to be making everybody else unhappy too.

At least when we got to Scotland we'd be able to escape from her for a bit. Whereas right now we were stuck in the van with hardly any music, one snoring toddler and a baby who, by the smell of it, had just filled his nappy.

It was a major relief when we finally pulled into the service station next to Dad's car. But it made us feel worse then ever when we entered the café and found Molly and Carli in sickeningly high spirits.

"We've had a wicked journey!" Molly gushed. "We've listened to two Westlife tapes and Robbie Williams. We even caught Dad singing along to them."

"Yeah, it was so funny I thought I was going to wet myself!"

"Carli!" Mum pretended to sound shocked. "What kind of journey have you lot had then? Noisy, I'll bet!"

"Erm, not exactly," I said truthfully, but I couldn't expand on that because Lyndz's mum had appeared looking tired and harassed.

"I didn't realise it was such a long way," she sighed, flopping down on the seat next to Mum's.

"Not to worry Patsy, the bulk of it's behind us now," Mum reassured her. "There's only a couple of hours to go."

"Two hours!" Frankie almost exploded. "I'm not sure I can stand that van for another two hours."

She said that last bit quietly because she didn't want Lyndz's mum to hear. It was true that the thought of two more hours cooped up with Mrs Trunchbull's more gruesome sister didn't seem a very exciting prospect. But it also meant that in two hours we'd be at Uncle Bob's place with a week of adventures in front of us!

In actual fact, the last two hours of the journey passed really quickly. It was very dark by the time we set off again, and we were soon in the countryside where there didn't seem to be too many streetlights. The darkness and the rhythm of the moving van seemed to make us all drowsy and I can't really remember anything much until Mr Collins suddenly shouted:

"Wake up guys! We're almost there!"

It was amazing, because one minute I was fast asleep and the next I was wide awake, staring eagerly out of the window.

For ages we couldn't really see anything.

We seemed to be driving up a long, long road with trees on one side and a huge expanse of water on the other.

"Look, a lake!" I pointed to it eagerly. "I knew there'd be a lake!"

Occasionally we caught sight of a startled pair of eyes on the road in front of us – rabbits, foxes, goodness knows what else.

"This is amazing!" breathed Mrs Collins softly.

Suddenly Mr Collins slowed down.

"Oh my goodness!" he gasped. "I didn't expect this!"

We all peered eagerly out of the windows. Looming before us beneath a sinister swirling mist was the creepiest, spookiest house I had ever seen in my life.

CHAPTER FIVE

"Th-this is a joke, right?" spluttered Fliss, stumbling from the van. "We're n-not really going to stay here, are we?"

I was kind of wondering whether it was one of Dad's jokes myself when the door of the house creaked open.

"A monster!" screeched Fliss and Rosie together, ducking down behind the van.

It was the funniest monster I'd ever seen. There in the doorway, silhouetted by the lights from the hall behind him, was a tiny little bloke dressed in a kilt and funny long socks. He was warbling *Scotland the Brave* and doing a strange little dance.

I saw Mum raise her eyes at Lyndz's mum. But miracle of miracles, Lyndz's mum was actually doubled over with laughter.

"Hello there, Bob!" Dad called out and climbed the steps to join him. "You've dressed the part for our Sassenach friends, I see!"

"Indeed laddie," Uncle Bob was shaking Dad's hand with gusto. "Can't be doing with the bairns thinking we Scots are a dour lot!"

"What's he talking about?" hissed Frankie in my ear. "I haven't understood one word. I didn't realise Scottish people spoke a different language!"

"Me neither," I agreed.

"Come in, come in," Uncle Bob gestured towards the rest of us. "You must be weary fit to drop. Mrs Barber's preparing the best hot chocolate north of the border, so come in and rest your bones a wee while afore bed."

"Come on girls, let's get you all inside." Lyndz's mum rounded us up with Ben asleep in one arm and Spike nodding off in the other. "This is going to be a fun week, I can just tell!"

We all exchanged glances. She was like a completely different person, all bubbly and bright like she used to be.

"It must be something in the air," I muttered.

"I'd better bottle some and take it home with us!" Lyndz giggled.

"I want to go home!" Fliss sobbed. "This place is just too – *weird*!"

"Come on Fliss, we're just tired, that's all," Frankie reassured her. "Things will look different in the morning – I promise!"

"I-if we're still here by then," Fliss stammered. "We'll probably have been b-bitten by a v-vampire or something!" And she burst into tears again.

"Now don't you worry about that, Fliss," I comforted her as I helped to carry her bag inside. "Frankie and I are expert vampire slayers, aren't we Franks? No big-toothed bloodsucker would *dare* mess with you, OK?"

I executed a few high kicks along with a bloodcurdling scream to prove my point.

Unfortunately the entrance hall was so vast that my scream sort of magnified and bounced off the walls. It sounded as though a mass-murderer was on the rampage in one of the rooms upstairs.

Frankie rolled her eyes at me as Fliss went off on another of her sob-fests.

"Now Kenny, you'll arouse the ghosties with noises like that!" Uncle Bob appeared in the hall in front of us. "This way for hot chocolate, then I'll show you all to your rooms."

We followed him in silence, trying to take in the vastness of the house. I know that I'd sort of dreamt that Uncle Bob lived in a castle, but I never thought it would be anything as enormous as this. The ceilings were so high that you had to strain your neck to look up at them. The walls were all wood-panelled with various deer heads mounted on plaques above us.

"Ooh, gross!" Frankie (the vegetarian) shuddered theatrically. "Killing animals like that is just disgusting!"

Fortunately Uncle Bob didn't seem to have heard. He led us into a room where an enormous fire roared in a massive stone fireplace. On a huge wooden table were steaming cups of the most gorgeous hot chocolate you have ever tasted in your life. Mmm, I can still taste it now – scrum-my!

"It looks to me like you all need your beds," Uncle Bob grinned as we were starting to doze by the fire. "Bairns first, follow me."

We all stared at him.

"He means you lot!" Dad laughed, pointing to Molly, Carli, my mates and me. "Off you go then, sleep well!"

Uncle Bob bounded up the stairs as we followed as quickly as we could, lugging our bags up with us.

"Here we have Molly and Carli's room." He flung open a door to reveal a pretty room with two enormous beds covered in rose-patterned eiderdowns. The curtains were all swagged and lamps cast a rosy glow.

"Cool!" Molly gasped.

Fliss looked in jealously. "It looks nice in there," she agreed. "I wouldn't mind sleeping in there myself!"

"With Molly?" Lyndz groaned. "You must be mad."

"Now I thought you lassies would all like to be together for your sleepover shenanigans," Uncle Bob told us as we walked a little further down the landing. "So I've put you all in here."

He flung open the door to reveal an absolutely ginormous room. It looked about as big as one of our classrooms. There were five beds all covered in sprigged bedspreads with a mountain of blankets underneath.

"I'll need a leg up to get in there!" Rosie giggled.

"The bathroom's just across the way," Uncle Bob pointed. "And don't you go minding the strange noises. Things tend to go bump in the night but it's usually only the hot water pipes. Nightie-night, sleep well."

He closed the door and left.

"I'm n-not sure about this." Fliss leant against her bed. "It's s-so s-spooky!"

"No it's not Fliss, it's exciting. Look at that!" I went to the far end of the room and pulled back the curtains. The night outside was thick and dark.

"Look at the moon! It's just—"

But I couldn't go on, because something had just flown past the window. It was something small and black, I was sure it was. I blinked hard. Maybe I was more tired than I thought and was imagining things. No, there was another one. Something with big wings. A shiver crept down my spine.

"What's up, Kenz?" Frankie demanded, coming to join me.

"I-I've just seen something fly past the window," I told her. "But I don't know what it was."

Fliss started howling and Rosie and Lyndz ran to comfort her.

"That's enough, Kenny," Frankie said sternly, snatching the curtains and drawing them together roughly. "You never know when to stop, do you? Fliss is already freaked out and you pull a stunt like that. Enough, OK?"

"But…" I protested, but I could tell by the look on Frankie's face that there was no point continuing.

"I'm sorry Fliss, I guess we're all a bit tired." I leapt up on to her bed. "I didn't mean to scare you – honest!"

Fliss sniffed and smiled weakly.

"Let's push the beds closer together so it feels more cosy," Lyndz suggested.

"Good idea, Batman," I agreed, and we heaved and shoved until they were all together at the end of the room nearest the door.

"Come on, let's get the bathroom stuff over with," Rosie suggested. "I don't know about you but I feel I could sleep for a week!"

"Well don't do that, Rosie-Posie," I punched her lightly on the arm. "'Cos we've got a week of Scottish fun ahead of us, remember!"

Now we might have had a week of excitement ahead of us, but that night was no picnic, I can tell you. Fliss was moaning and shivering on one side of me, and Lyndz was snoring her head off opposite. Fun it was not. We didn't even have a midnight feast because we were so tired. I was glad when it was morning so we could start to explore.

Over a mammoth breakfast of porridge and toast Uncle Bob told us, "Just you lassies make yourselves at home. It's good to have some young blood in the house again."

"Do you reckon *he's* a vampire then?" I whispered to Frankie.

She just mouthed, "You idiot!" and whacked my leg under the table.

"Just steer clear of the loch, it is very deep," Uncle Bob continued. "And it might be sensible to come inside when it starts dropping dark – you can see all sorts of shapes lurking among the trees at dusk. I wouldn'ae want you to be scared now!"

Fliss gasped and looked very anxious again.

"He is joking Fliss," Mum said firmly, frowning as Uncle Bob left the room. "But I don't want you roaming about in the dark anyway, it can get very cold. Just go and amuse yourselves quietly and we'll see you back here for lunch at one."

We all ran off, whooping and hollering. The first room we discovered was a library lined with books from floor to ceiling.

"Wow!" breathed Frankie. "I didn't think one person could own so many books!"

Then we practised skidding down the hallway in our socks for ages, until Ben found us and wanted to join in.

"'Snot fair!" he whimpered as Lyndz's mum scooped him up and carried him away.

"Sorry girls!" she called over her shoulder.

"Your mum certainly seems a lot happier!" Rosie said.

"I know!" Lyndz grinned. "She said she'd had the best night's sleep she's had in months. And she's really excited about helping to get everything ready for the party too. It's great!"

It certainly was great to see Lyndz looking so much happier too.

Running upstairs we could hear music thumping out of Molly and Carli's room.

"We come all this way and they stay in their room listening to tapes!" I tutted. "They could do that anywhere. How could they pass up the chance to explore this great house?"

"Where do you suppose this leads?" asked Fliss, turning a door handle. "It's not one of the bedrooms."

She opened the door a crack and we peered into the darkness.

"There are some stairs," said Rosie excitedly. "It must lead to the attic!"

We all looked at each other and shrieked, "Jeanne!" Then we burst out laughing.

We must have told you about the time we stayed in a hotel in Paris and nearly scared ourselves stupid because we thought someone was being held prisoner in the attic?

"I hope exploring up here's not going to be as terrifying as last time!" Fliss shivered. "At least there's no creepy maid this time. Boy, was that Chantal scary!"

"Wasn't she just!" Rosie laughed.

We'd reached the top of the stairs and the attic looked pretty empty.

"No prisoners here!" Frankie announced.

"Only that blimming noise from Molly's stupid tapes!" I snarled.

"If we follow the noise we can work out where her room is!" Frankie suggested.

"Excellent!"

The attic itself was vast with not much in

it at all, just a few piles of dusty papers and some empty packing cases. We crept silently along, occasionally stopping to listen to the noises below us.

"Listen, I can hear Mum talking to Spike," Lyndz whispered. "We must be above the boys' room."

"And we're definitely getting nearer to Molly's room," Fliss whispered. "The noise is getting louder."

We crept on a little further until we were standing directly over the music. The floor felt as though it was moving slightly from the vibrations.

"I'm surprised she's not deaf listening to it that loud!" Rosie murmured.

"If we leap up and down she'll probably think it's part of the song!" Lyndz laughed.

"Well she would if we did it now!" I grinned. "But it wouldn't half give her a shock if we did it in the middle of the night!"

"You wouldn't!" Fliss looked part shocked, part scared.

"Well let's just say – it depends," I told them thoughtfully. "But, just in case, we'd better mark out exactly where Molly's room is."

We dragged a couple of packing cases over to roughly mark out the boundaries.

"Now if that sister of mine pulls just *one* stunt this week," I told the others firmly, "we're going to let her have it – big time!"

CHAPTER SIX

All the time we were having lunch we kept eyeballing Molly and Carli and laughing.

"Grow up!" Molly yelled at last. "You're just so immature! Ignore them, Carli."

"Molly for goodness sake, we've come away on holiday! Can't you and Laura forget your differences for once?" Mum snapped.

"Not likely!"

"Well there's plenty of room for you to stay out of each other's way then," Mum replied tartly. "And it might not do you and Carli any harm to get some fresh air. You can listen to your tapes any time. The air is so clean here, you ought to make the most of it before we go home."

Molly rolled her eyes and made a being-sick face behind Mum's back. Then she turned to me.

"You're dead!" she muttered before stomping out, with Carli in close pursuit.

"I'm so scared!" I pretended to quake in my shoes.

"What have you girls got planned for this afternoon?" asked Lyndz's mum.

"Exploring outside!"

"Well don't stay out too late," Mum warned us. "It gets dark a bit earlier up here. And for goodness sake, stay out of trouble!"

"Mother!" I looked at her innocently. "We *always* stay out of trouble!"

"If only I could believe that!" Mum sighed.

We grabbed our coats and, whooping and yelling, ran like mad things to the edge of the lake (or "loch" as Uncle Bob called it).

"It's amazing!" Fliss breathed. "It looks like something out of a fairytale!"

"That it is, Felicity!" Uncle Bob had appeared silently behind us. "If ever I have any troubles, I bring myself here and they all seem to sort themselves out."

"I could sort out all my troubles by pushing Molly into the loch," I grumbled. "And holding her under!"

Uncle Bob laughed. He picked a few stones from the ground, then one by one he skimmed them across the lake so that they bounced along the surface, once, twice, even three times.

"That's wicked!" Rosie gasped. "Could you teach us how to do that?"

"I reckon so!" he smiled. "First you've got to find nice flat stones – not too small and not too big."

We hunted at our feet.

"Now then, stand at an angle to the loch and focus. The action's all in the wrist. Relax, then whip it, like this."

His stone skimmed the lake in four easy bounces.

"Now you try!"

Our stones just plopped in.

"Try again!"

Uncle Bob encouraged us and helped us

with our aim. Just when we were starting to get a bit bored, Fliss's stone skipped twice along the lake's surface.

"I did it, I did it!" She leapt up and down.

That spurred us on to try harder and eventually we all managed it. It felt fantastic, a real sense of achievement!

"It's a wee bit nippy!" Uncle Bob shivered. "But I know what'll warm you up!"

He led us away from the lake to a clearing where Dad and Mr Collins were sawing logs.

"I've got us some helpers!" he grinned.

Dad looked apprehensive. "I'm not sure about that Bob, saws can be pretty dangerous."

"Och, not when I'm supervising. Calm yourself, Jim," Uncle Bob replied.

First Frankie and I had a go at sawing, then Lyndz and Fliss. Finally Rosie had a go with Uncle Bob. When we weren't sawing we were helping to stack up the logs in great piles. I'd never got so hot, nor ached so much in my life, not even playing football.

"Right lassies, it's almost dusk now!" Uncle Bob told us at last. "Time for a wee romp outside afore it's time to go in. I'd check out the chapel by the loch if I were you. I've heard tell of great goings-on down there at about this time. You must have a look – if you're brave enough, that is!"

"W-what does he mean?" Fliss looked at us anxiously as we walked away towards the lake again.

"Ah, nothing, Fliss! You should know by now that Uncle Bob's just a big wind-up merchant. He just wants to tease us, that's all," I reassured her.

But as we approached the lake I wasn't so sure. The light seemed to have faded in just a short time and everything seemed to be casting freaky shadows around us. The wind was whistling through the trees, twisting the branches into sinister shapes.

"I don't like this!" Fliss hung back. "Let's go back to the house – please!"

"We'll just have a quick look at the chapel first," I promised.

A dark shell of a building stood between the lake and the house, its roof caving in and its walls starting to crumble.

"Oooh, well spooky!" Frankie shuddered.

We stopped a little way from it, too scared to go any nearer.

"D-did you see that?" Lyndz gasped suddenly. "I'm sure I just saw a shadow moving about in there!"

"And a flash of light," I mumbled.

"I can hear strange noises," Rosie shuddered. "Let's get out of here!"

I was starting to feel knotted up and sick inside. This really was a bit too scary. Fliss was shaking and crying.

"I want to go home," she sobbed. "This is frightening me now."

I tried to pull myself together.

"Now what would Buffy do in a situation like this?" I asked. "She wouldn't wimp out, would she?"

I took a deep breath and did a few high kicks and karate moves with my arms. I tried to yell something fierce but my voice came out in a reedy wail.

Suddenly a twig cracked behind me and I sensed someone watching me from the shadows. Instinctively I lashed back with my left leg and swung round with my right arm.

"Watch it, you moron!"

"MOLLY!" we all yelled together.

She stepped into the clearing, clutching her side where my foot had caught her. She flashed a torch on the others.

"Mum told me I had to come out here and find you," she snarled. "I wish I hadn't bothered!"

"It was you!" Rosie and Frankie gasped in relief.

"Thought you'd scare us, did you?" I snarled back, the strength flooding back into my voice. "Well, you'll have to do better than that!"

"What are they on about, Molly?" Carli looked puzzled.

"Don't come the innocent!" I snapped. "We're on to you two!"

Molly tapped her head with her finger and pulled a face at Carli.

"Mental!" she mouthed.

Boy was I mad! I swear that I'd have strangled her there and then if Mum hadn't appeared to round us up for supper.

Mrs Barber, with a little help from Mum and Mrs Collins, had prepared this amazing meal. We started with thick soup. Then she brought out these enormous *wild-boar* sausages and huge bowls of mashed potato. It was the best I'd ever tasted, I could live on it forever! The sausages were kind of strong-tasting but good. Fliss and Rosie weren't too keen, but fortunately Mrs Barber had prepared a vegetable casserole for Frankie because she doesn't eat meat, so they shared that. For pudding it was treacle tart and custard – *fan-tastic*!

We all helped Mrs Barber to clear away, then we went to flop in the lounge where we'd had hot chocolate the night before. Uncle Bob lit loads of candles and the adults sat on the big squashy sofas whilst the rest of us lay around on the floor by the fire. It was wicked, especially when Uncle Bob started telling us all these spooky stories.

"Some say you can hear a wailing in a chapel not too far from here," he told us in a voice so low that you had to strain your ears to hear him. "It belongs to Flora McDonald.

The poor wee lassie turned up on her wedding day to discover that her fiancé had been killed in a hunting accident. She went mad with grief and killed herself right there in front of the altar. If you listen hard you can hear the swish of her wedding dress as her ghost wanders through the chapel. Some have even seen a figure dressed in white wandering through the grounds."

"AHH!" Fliss screamed. "Not here? Not the chapel we went to today?"

"No, not that chapel, Fliss," Mum said very firmly. "Not *any* chapel, right Uncle Bob? These are just folktales, aren't they? And ones that aren't very suitable just before bedtime if I might say so!"

"Aye, you're right, Valerie," Uncle Bob grinned. "Don't mind an old fool with more tales to tell than sense. Now Felicity, I didn'ae mean to upset you. How about hot chocolate all round, Mrs Barber?"

"I think we'll take ours to our room with us if that's OK," I said when Mrs Barber appeared back with a tray full of steaming mugs. The others looked at me, amazed.

"We're very tired, aren't we?" I stared at them hard.

"Oh yes, 'course, all that sawing you know!" Frankie followed my lead. "Night everybody!"

The others followed us out of the sitting room and we all trooped upstairs to our bedroom.

"Couldn't we have stayed downstairs a bit longer?" Fliss asked apprehensively. "You know, with the others."

"No Fliss, we've got business to attend to," I told her, leaping on to my bed. "Molly and Carli business. They scared us outside, remember, so now it's payback time!"

I pointed to the attic. The others squashed on to my bed and, huddling together, we formed our grand plan. When it was all sorted we did high fives and ran giggling into the bathroom. It was important that we were ready to go as soon as we figured that Molly and Carli were settled down for the night.

It seemed like about five hours before they even came up to bed, and another hour before they'd finished in the bathroom.

"What are they *doing* in there?" Frankie sounded exasperated.

"Molly's so ugly she needs about a million potions to hold her face together," I snorted. "One day it'll probably crack up completely and fall off!"

By the time they'd emerged from the bathroom Lyndz had dozed off so we had to wake her up.

"Wassup!" she grumbled.

"Come on, sleepy-head. It's action time!"

We crept to the door. I was just about to reach for the handle when I could hear footsteps along the passageway.

"It sounds like everybody else is coming to bed now!" I grumbled.

We crept back into bed and had to wait again until we were sure that the coast was clear.

"Everybody ready?" I whispered as we huddled for a second time behind the door. "Everybody know what we're supposed to be doing?"

With excited butterflies chasing about in my tummy I reached for the door handle.

Instead of the door creaking open, as I'd expected, the handle shot off in my hand! There was a *clunk* on the landing as the knob on the other side fell off too.

"What's happened?" asked Fliss anxiously.

"Erm, it's not looking good actually," I admitted, brandishing the knob. "We're stuck in here, and I can't see how we're going to get out."

CHAPTER SEVEN

"It's that ghost!" wailed Fliss. "Flora McDonald has come to haunt us!"

"Don't be so stupid!" I snapped. "There's got to be some perfectly sensible explanation..."

Frankie was crouched by the door, squinting through the keyhole.

"You know that perfectly sensible explanation?" she said at last, straightening herself up. "I think it's called Molly and Carli! They're on the other side of the door looking like the cats who got the cream!"

"They'll look like cats who've got the SCREAM when I get hold of them!" I fumed.

"But first we need to get out of here."

I pushed the door again, but there was no way it was going to budge.

"HELP!" Rosie and Fliss started banging on the door. "Get us out of here!"

"Love to help you!" Molly said from the other side of the door. "We can't open it from this side either. I wonder how that could have happened?"

"Yes, I wonder, young lady!" There was no mistaking Mum's voice and she sounded A-N-G-R-Y!

"But Mum!" Molly didn't sound so smug now. "It's nothing to do with us!"

"Molly, it's too late for silly games. I want that door open and I want you to get back to bed!"

"I really think it's a job for a locksmith," Lyndz's dad announced seriously.

"They'll never get one so late!" Frankie hissed. "We're going to be stuck in here all night!"

"I knew this place was doomed!" Fliss sobbed. "There's something really creepy about it."

"Now I think that's just your imagination, Felicity!"

We all spun round to see Uncle Bob grinning at us from the far corner of the room. He had suddenly appeared. Out of thin air. The door hadn't opened and the window was closed so there was no way he could have got in there…

We all took one look at him and started screaming. We clung together shrieking our heads off like we were in some really bad horror movie. And all the time Uncle Bob was watching us with this silly grin on his face. At last he chuckled:

"Girls, girls, please! There's no need to be alarmed."

"B-but how did you get in?" I squeaked nervously as soon as I'd recovered my voice. The guy was freaking me out big time.

"There's a secret doorway here, look!"

He pressed against one of the panels on the wall and it sprung open, revealing a door.

"That's amazing! Like something out of a film!" Frankie said open-mouthed, hurrying to see where it led.

"It goes into the bedroom next door," Uncle Bob explained. "That's why I gave you this room. I thought maybe your Sleepover Club might discover it for yourselves."

Suddenly Uncle Bob wasn't spooky any more. He just seemed like a little guy with a wicked sense of fun.

"*You* didn't take the doorknob off so we'd find out about this, did you?" I asked him.

"No Kenny, I wouldn'ae go to all that trouble, believe me!" he grinned. "I suggest you leave this door open tonight, just in case the doorknob gremlin decides to have another go. Although I doubt she'd dare, the mood your mother's in!"

We all laughed. Outside our room we could still hear Mum tearing a strip off Molly.

"Have a good rest now. Goodnight!" He left as quietly as he'd arrived.

Even though it was very late by the time Mum and Lyndz's mum had been in to check that we were all right, we were still wide awake.

"I guess we'll just have to have a midnight feast!" I shrugged, pretending it was just about the last thing on earth that we wanted to do.

We grabbed mini-Snickers, fizzy lollies, a carton of Pringles and mini cans of marshmallow soda from our bags and piled on to Frankie's bed.

"I thought I'd die when your Uncle Bob appeared!" giggled Rosie. "My heart stopped beating, I swear!"

"He's a pretty cool guy, isn't he?" I grinned.

"I still think he's weird!" Fliss moaned.

We all bombarded her with crisps and sweets.

"Gitoutofit!" She threw them back at us. "I mean, you have to admit it's pretty strange how he keeps appearing behind us without us even hearing him."

"He's just light on his feet," I told her. "And remember, that's exactly what *we* have to be when we get our revenge on Molly in the attic."

I was so pumped up that I would happily have gone into the attic there and then, but Frankie persuaded me that it would be more sensible to wait.

"Your mum's pretty wound up at the moment, Kenz," she reasoned. "And if she caught us pulling a stunt like that tonight she'd go into meltdown!"

I reckoned the next day was bound to drag as we waited to put our plan into action. WRONG! It actually flashed past, because we made the most *amazing* discovery when we retraced our steps from the previous evening.

"We're not going back to the chapel, are we?" Fliss looked alarmed. "You don't really think Flora McDonald's ghost will be there, do you?"

"Don't be daft Fliss, there're no such things as ghosts," I reassured her. "What *I'm* interested in are the vampires."

"WHAT?" Fliss looked like she was about to faint.

I ploughed on. "Look, we heard noises right, round an old chapel? And where does Buffy do her vampire-slaying? In a graveyard, right? Well, I reckon there might well be graves round that old chapel and I think it would be an ideal hanging-out spot for those

Scottish vamps. Especially now they've heard that there are two slayers on the scene."

I did a ferocious side-kick to prove my point. "Eh Frankie, what do you say? Do you reckon they want to try their luck with us? Maybe this is Sunnydale Mark Two!"

"You're mad!" Lyndz and Rosie were shaking their heads. "You don't really believe all that stuff, do you?"

"Sure thing!" I nodded. "Come on, I bet we can find some signs of vampire activity last night."

We got to the edge of the woods, then crept cautiously towards the chapel. It wasn't as scary as it had been the night before, but there was still something a bit eerie about the place.

"Right everyone, look out for signs," I hissed.

As we approached the chapel we all stooped close to the ground.

"What exactly are we looking for?" asked Fliss weakly.

"Footprints. Like this one!" I pointed excitedly to the ground.

There in the earth were footprints, enormous ones.

"Those weren't made by Molly and Carli, were they?" Rosie looked scared.

"There are more," Frankie pointed, "and they're all leading to the chapel."

We followed them right to the entrance of the building.

"Hey, what's this?" Lyndz bent down and picked up something from among the weeds on the ground.

"It's a c-cross!" she squealed, opening her palm so we could all see it.

A gold-coloured cross, streaked with mud, glinted faintly in the sunshine.

"You know what this means," I told the others firmly. "Someone must have been trying to protect themselves against the vampires by holding this up – then they got scared and ran away."

Fliss and Rosie made some weedy gulping noises. I moved further into the chapel to take a closer look. Frankie and Lyndz came with me, whilst Fliss and Rosie hung round the door.

"What's that?" Lyndz whispered, pointing up to a dark shape hanging from the exposed beams of the ceiling.

"Dunno." Frankie went to inspect further. Then she went kind of pale and started to back out of the chapel.

"Bats!" she shrieked when she was by the door. "Loads of them!"

We started screaming and running all at the same time.

When we were back at the house we collapsed in our bedroom. Thank goodness we could lock the door this time – the locksmith had sorted out the problem.

"Everything adds up," I gasped. "The noises we heard, the cross, the bats. I reckon we did stumble upon some vampires the other night."

"Shouldn't we tell someone?" Fliss asked frantically.

"No way! Besides, I think Uncle Bob knows," I told them. "Remember how he told us to go to the chapel? Maybe he's testing us out. We've got to get ourselves prepared with crosses and stakes and go down there and slay ourselves some vampires!"

"Not tonight?" Rosie looked alarmed.

"Nope, tonight we've got another mission to accomplish," I reminded them. "Tonight we're going to scare Molly and Carli witless!"

You know when you're really up for something but you've got to wait for the right time to do it? Well, it's like time goes on strike, isn't it? Every minute just stretches out in front of you. Even listening to Uncle Bob's stories wasn't so much fun because we were so keen to get on with some action of our own.

We went to bed ahead of everyone else and ran through our plan one last time. Then it was just a case of waiting until Molly and Carli came upstairs before we could sneak out to the attic.

"What if Ben and Spike wake up? Mum might rumble what we're up to." Lyndz looked anxious. "And she's been so great since she's been here, I don't want her relapsing into one of her moods again."

"Look Lyndz, that's a chance we'll have to take," I said firmly. "We know where the boys' bedroom is – we'll just have to make extra sure that we don't make any sound when we walk over it. Ready?"

The others nodded. "Ready."

We wrapped ourselves in our dressing gowns and crept out into the passageway. The others crept towards the door leading to the attic and I went to Molly and Carli's room.

"Mum says you're to turn off your tape and go to sleep NOW!" I shouted through the door. "She's still mad with you about our bedroom door. And if you don't shut up she says you'll have to miss out on the party."

"You creep!" Molly yelled back, but within seconds she'd turned off her music and the lamps.

"We'd better do what the scumbag says," I heard Molly whisper. "She'll probably grass us up otherwise, and there's no way I'm missing that party!"

I put my thumbs up to the others and crept to join them.

Now I'm glad that we have torches as part of our sleepover kit, because we certainly needed them up there in the attic. It was so dark you just couldn't see anything in front of you. And cold too! Somehow it seemed so much bigger than it had done in the daytime.

"We must be there by now!" whispered Rosie. "Are you sure we haven't passed the packing cases we used to mark out Molly's room?"

"No way!"

"Listen!" Lyndz suddenly hissed. "Isn't that Spike crying?"

We all held our breath. If Lyndz's mum came to check on him, as sure as eggs is eggs she'd check on us too. Molly wasn't the only one who might be missing the party!

"It's OK, I think he must just be having a dream," Lyndz sighed with relief when there was silence below us again.

"Well at least we know that Molly's room isn't too far away," Frankie whispered. "Look, the cases are here."

We tiptoed to the middle of them and grinned at each other.

"Let's do it!"

Frankie and I took off our dressing gowns and started to drag them over the floor, making a loud swishing sound. Fliss and Rosie danced and stamped around whilst Lyndz moaned and groaned.

To begin with, we thought Molly and Carli must be asleep because there was no sound below us. Then we heard a low urgent murmuring. We stopped where we were, then started again – swishing, stamping and moaning. It was all going fantastically – until Lyndz's moans were joined by loud "hic!"s. She'd got the dreaded hiccups!

"No Lyndz!" I almost shouted, running over to her and clamping my hand over her mouth. "You'll give the game away."

By that time we could hear anxious sobs below us.

"Time we were gone!" I whispered to the others.

We hurried to the stairway as quickly and quietly as we could. Turning to the others I laughed, "Go on, tell me that wasn't our best yet!"

But no-one spoke. They looked terrified. I spun round to see what the problem was – only to be met by the shadowy figure of a man looming up the stairs towards us.

CHAPTER EIGHT

I took one look at the lumbering form and started to scream. I wanted to run back up to the attic, but my legs had turned to jelly.

"Away with your screaming," chuckled the figure, emerging out of the shadows. "Anyone would think you'd seen a ghost!"

"Uncle Bob!" we gasped in unison.

"You see!" sobbed Fliss. "He keeps appearing without us hearing anything."

"Fliss!"

"Well it's weird! And scary!"

But there was something much scarier coming up the main stairs – MUM! She was on the warpath, wanting to find out what all the commotion was about. Molly and Carli were outside their bedroom weeping and wailing about spooky sounds in the attic. Mum was bound to see us and put two and two together – she's very good at that kind of maths.

Uncle Bob motioned for us to hurry along the landing and closed the attic door behind us. As Mum rounded the corner, we were almost back outside our own bedroom.

"Ah, there you are, Valerie," he greeted Mum warmly. "I found these wee lassies terrified out of their wits. They say something has been making a proper din up there." He pointed to the attic. "It must be Headless Eric doing his rounds again. He's the house ghost; a noisy wee thing but he's harmless enough. Wouldn'ae hurt a flea."

Mum looked at us suspiciously so we tried to look as terrified as possible.

"D-did you hear it too?" Frankie stammered as Molly and Carli appeared, trembling and shaking. "Wasn't it gruesome?"

They both nodded, and it took me all my time not to burst out laughing. Respect to

Frankie, she played an absolute blinder. They were totally convinced that we really *had* been scared by Headless Eric!

"I'll hear no more talk of ghosts!" said Mum sternly, ushering us back to our rooms. "There must be a perfectly sensible explanation for the noises."

She stared hard at Uncle Bob as she spoke. He just carried on smiling, but as soon as her back was turned he gave me a great big wink and the cheekiest grin!

When Mum had finally gone back downstairs I nearly exploded.

"Isn't Uncle Bob just the most fun?" I grinned, tossing a handful of fizzy fish at the others. "I mean, how many other adults would have got us out of that mess?"

"He certainly is one barmy old dude!" agreed Lyndz, whose hiccups had disappeared in the excitement.

Fliss didn't say anything, she just sat on her bed chewing her sweet thoughtfully.

"But you were pretty awesome too, Frankie," Rosie reminded us. "Talk about thinking on your feet!"

Frankie stood up on her bed.

"I thank you all, my humble servants!" She bowed elaborately.

"No need to get carried away!" I said, thwacking her with my pillow.

We hadn't had a pillow fight for ages so the others joined in. Wicked!

Afterwards, as we lay exhausted on our beds, I told the others, "If we put as much energy into our vampire-slaying, those demons won't stand a chance!"

"Aw man, can't we have a break from all that?" Rosie moaned. "This holiday is turning out to be pretty exhausting."

"Look Rosie-Posie, we're on a mission," I told her firmly. "And we cannot fail."

I had intended to go on our vampire patrol the very next night, but we set out in the morning to do the touristy sightseeing thing and it was dark when we arrived back. However much we pleaded, there was no way that Mum was going to let us "roam about outside", as she put it.

The next day, party-frenzy hit town. We had

to help tidy up this room and help trim up that. And just when we thought it was safe to go outside, Uncle Bob got us to help move all the furniture around. Typical!

The same thing happened the following day too. As soon as the light was beginning to fade and we were about to head out of the door, Uncle Bob called us back.

"Ah there you are now," he chuckled. "I was hoping you'd be able to help me with these."

He produced a bag containing about a million balloons.

"We want the place looking nice and cheerful for the party, don't we now?"

"Couldn't we do that tomorrow, Uncle Bob?" I pleaded. "The party isn't until Saturday. We've still got two days left. "

"Ah now, there's all the cooking to do tomorrow, Kenny," he told me with a gleam in his eye. "And you don't want to miss out on the haggis-making, do you?"

He handed over the balloons.

"Kenny's the right one for that job!" Molly called out snidely as she and Carli walked past. "She's full of hot air!"

I could have strangled her. But Uncle Bob went one better – he made them dust all the books in his library! Classic!

"It's almost like your uncle doesn't want us to go outside, isn't it?" Rosie said, taking a breather from blowing up balloons. "Do you think he's got something to hide?"

"I don't know," I replied, thoughtfully. "But we're definitely going to find out tomorrow night."

In preparation for our vampire-slaying mission we went to bed early and made crosses from pieces of wood which we'd found in a box next to the fireplace in the lounge.

"Do you think these are going to work?" Fliss asked, holding up a very wonky-looking cross held together with Sellotape.

"Deffo," I assured her. "It's the *symbol* of the cross that vampires are scared of, it doesn't matter what they're made of."

I sharpened a few sticks as best I could with the help of Fliss's nail file.

"Look, I've got myself some stakes too! Bring on the vampires!"

But that night it wasn't vampires we had to deal with, but Headless Eric again. Or at least, that's what Molly and Carli would have liked us to believe. At about two o'clock in the morning I felt someone shaking me.

"Wassup!" I mumbled crossly. "Leave me alone will you?"

I looked up to see Fliss and Rosie staring at me.

"Listen!" Rosie whispered.

At first I couldn't hear anything. Then there was a scraping and moaning noise above us.

"It's c-coming from the attic!" Fliss stammered. "Do you think it really is Headless Eric?"

"Don't be daft!" I told her. "That was just Uncle Bob's story to get us out of trouble. It's got to be Molly, she must be stupid if she thought we'd fall for that trick ourselves."

"You mean she sussed it was us?" Frankie asked. She and Lyndz were now sitting on my bed with the others.

"Must have!" I shrugged. "Come on, let's go and sort her out!"

We crept to the door and out on to the

landing. We were halfway along to the attic door when all the lights were turned on.

"Sprung!" Mum announced viciously.

Molly and Carli were just in front. They looked absolutely amazed when they caught sight of us.

"Now I don't know who it was that rigged up that little charade," Mum was looking from me to Molly, "but it's beyond a joke. Nobody believes in ghosts, OK? And if there's any more mischief like that, you'll all be grounded and none of you will be going to the party on Saturday, is that understood?"

"But that's not f—" Molly began.

"*Is that understood?*" Mum repeated firmly.

"Yes!" We all nodded glumly.

"Now back to bed, all of you!" Mum watched as we headed back to our bedrooms.

As Molly passed behind us she hissed, "We'll get you back for that!"

"What did she mean?" Rosie asked crossly when we back in bed. "*They* were the ones pretending to be Headless Eric this time."

"I just want to know how they got back from the attic so quickly," Frankie yawned sleepily.

Hmm, that certainly was a mystery. But I could tap Molly for that information later. We only had one more chance to slay the vampires before we went home, and I was determined that nothing was going to mess that up.

All the next day we were as helpful as possible – fetching, carrying, peeling and chopping. We figured that if we worked our socks off all day, nobody could refuse us the chance to cut loose for a little while in the evening. And as we were in the kitchen I had the perfect opportunity to 'borrow' a little garlic – vampires *hate* that!

By late afternoon, the kitchen was groaning with food. There was just one last dish to prepare – haggis!

"What on earth is haggis anyway?" Fliss asked.

"Well," Mrs Barber grinned. "As Robbie Burns once wrote, it's the 'Great Chieftain o' the puddin' race'."

"Pudding, great! Count us in!"

Mum and Lyndz's mum exchanged weird looks.

"Well you'd better help me with the

ingredients then," Mrs Barber smiled, leading the way to the fridge.

Frankie took one look inside and dashed outside with her hand over her mouth.

"Gonna hurl!" she moaned.

Fliss and Rosie ran after her. Lyndz and I stayed to have a closer look.

"Och, the girl's gone soft. Has she never seen a sheep's heart and liver before?" Mrs Barber pretended to look amazed.

"And w-what's that?" Lyndz asked, pointing to another bloody-looking container lurking inside the fridge.

"Why that's the sheep's lungs!" Mrs Barber explained, removing the container. "And this here's the sheep's paunch, or stomach bag. We mix up all those goodies with oatmeal, onions and seasoning, then stuff it back in here and boil it. It's the most delicious thing you'll ever taste."

Lyndz had gone a funny shade of green. And I was feeling none too clever myself.

"Why don't you two run along and see if Frankie's OK?" Lyndz's mum ushered us out of the kitchen. "You've worked ever so hard today, go and get some fresh air whilst we finish up in here."

We didn't need telling twice. We ran and ran until we finally caught up with the others leaning against a tree outside.

"You OK?" I asked Frankie.

"Mm," she nodded. "It was all that bloody stuff, it was disgusting." She went pale again at the thought of it.

"You don't suppose your Uncle Bob really is a vampire himself, do you?" asked Rosie. "And that was the remains of one of his victims?"

Fliss squealed.

"Nah!" I shook my head. "But speaking of vampires, look it's getting dark. This might be our last chance to slay them. Let's go upstairs, grab our things and prepare to do battle."

We charged up to our room, stuffed the crosses, stakes and garlic into our pockets and ran outside again. Uncle Bob was just walking up to the house.

"You're brave venturing out there," he grinned. "You want to be careful, you never know what you might meet."

We all looked at each other and he went inside, rubbing his hands and chuckling to himself.

"There's something going on here and I don't l-like it," Fliss shivered. "Let's go back inside."

"Look Fliss, do you want to come with *us* or stuff disgusting muck into a sheep's stomach?" I asked her. "The choice is yours."

Felicity remained rooted to the spot.

"Felicity Proudlove, you are the weakest link, goodbye!"

We started to walk away towards the chapel.

"No, don't leave me!" she yelled and came hurtling after us.

"We'll be OK if we stick together," I told everyone firmly.

When we had the chapel in our sights we went in single file, creeping carefully and trying to make as little noise as possible.

As soon as we got to the chapel, we knew we were not alone. Something was moving about on the other side. Torches occasionally flashed, and there was a low murmuring of voices. I peeped through the open doorway and saw a hooded figure. I gasped and pulled back.

"There's something round the other side," I whispered to the others. "We'll have to creep round. It's too dark to go in here."

"I want to go home!" Fliss sobbed. "Please let's go back."

"I'm with Fliss," Rosie agreed. "Come on, this could be dangerous!"

My heart was pounding in my chest. And I admit that I was scared. Really scared. Part of me wanted to turn and run. But part of me thought: *Come on Kenny, this is exciting*!

Besides, I knew that the others would never let me forget it if they thought for one second that I was as terrified as they were.

"You stay here if you want," I hissed. "But I'm going in!"

I hugged the wall of the chapel as I crept stealthily round to the other side. Frankie was right behind me – I could hear her breathing down my neck. And Lyndz was behind her.

When we got to the corner I turned and whispered, "Get your stakes ready. On a count of three, let's get slaying. One, two, THREE!"

We rushed out like mad things, yelling and screaming at the tops of our voices. I executed a few high kicks, although at first I couldn't really see what I was aiming for, it was too dark.

Then I saw the figures again. There were lots more than I'd expected. I ran towards them with my cross raised, brandishing my garlic. I tried to do a flying drop kick just like Buffy, but it wasn't that easy. I seemed to get my legs all wrong and landed awkwardly. I tried to recover myself, but as I staggered to my feet something grabbed me from behind and dragged me into some bushes.

"Help! Frankie! Lyndz!" I yelled. But it was no good – *they'd got them too*!

CHAPTER NINE

"Leggoofme!" I yelled, thrashing about with my arms and legs. All I could see were these dark shapes surrounding me.

"Ouch!" I made contact with something, it felt like a shin. Whatever I'd kicked was obviously reeling in pain, so I tried more of the same.

"Och, you little wild beastie!" a man's voice snarled crossly. "Put the torch on her, Andrew!"

Now I'll admit that up until then, I was convinced that I was fighting for my life. We'd been captured by vampires who were going to kill us for sure. But that voice didn't sound as though it belonged to a vampire – and I'd certainly never heard of a vampire calling itself *Andrew*!

A bright light suddenly flashed on to my face. I blinked and tried to turn away from it. The first thing I saw was Frankie struggling furiously against two men who were holding her by the shoulders. Next to her a woman was grappling with Lyndz. They were all wearing jeans and anoraks. Now I know that vampires are masters of disguise – but *anoraks*? Per-lease!

"Just what on earth do you think you are doing?" asked the man behind me furiously. "Your silly games could easily disturb the bats and that's exactly what we're trying to avoid."

"Bats?" We all spoke together.

"Yes, we're here observing the bat colony in the chapel," said the woman. She was quite young and fortunately she didn't seem as cross as the other man. In fact she looked as though she was desperately trying to stop laughing.

"We've been here all week trying to establish approximately how many bats there are," she continued. "Whether they're in good health and how far advanced they are in their preparations for hibernation."

"Bats!" I repeated like an idiot. "We thought you were vampires!"

Everyone just cracked up. Talk about *us* disturbing the bat population! They made so much noise they probably disturbed every bat from Scotland to the South of France!

"Now, now. Don't mock the girls. I thought they showed great spirit!" Uncle Bob had appeared with Fliss and Rosie. They were all grinning from ear to ear.

"That was so funny!" Rosie was laughing so much she was almost choking. "You ought to have seen yourself, Kenny!"

"Can it, Rosie!" I snarled. "You knew about this all the time didn't you, Uncle Bob? Why didn't you tell us that there were bat-watchers here?"

"And spoil all your fun?" Uncle Bob grinned. "Now I couldn'ae do that, Kenny.

Look, no harm's done and now you're here you can watch the bats too."

He pointed overhead. The air was filled with black shapes sweeping out into the sky from the chapel. Once they'd soared higher, they seemed to swoop down suddenly.

"Eek, my hair! They'll get stuck in my hair!" squealed Fliss and put her hands protectively over her head.

"The last thing bats would do is land in your hair." The older man still sounded really annoyed with us.

"It's true," the woman told us gently. "They're swooping like that to feed on insects. They have to eat as many as possible at the moment because soon they'll be hibernating for winter so they're in the process of fattening up. Even these tiny bats can eat up to 3,000 insects at one feeding."

"Really?" I was totally stunned. "That's awesome!"

"But how can they see in the dark?" asked Lyndz.

"Well actually they don't," Andrew, the guy who'd flashed the torch in my face, explained. "They use a system of echo-location. That just means that as they fly, they make high-pitched sounds. They find out what obstacles are in their way by the echoes they get back. Clever, huh?"

"Wicked!"

"You know when I said I'd seen something flying past our window on the day we got here?" I told the others excitedly. "It must have been a bat! But I always thought bats were a lot bigger than these ones?"

"Oh they can be," the woman explained. "These are pipistrelles. They're the smallest and most common bats in Britain. They only weigh about seven grammes, tops."

"Wow!" breathed Frankie. "That's tiny!"

When we were sure that all the bats had left the chapel we crept to the doorway to take a peek inside. There was a faint high-pitched noise, coming for somewhere.

"Careful everyone," the man told us. "It sounds like there's a bat in trouble."

We shone our torches on to the beams and over the ground.

"Look!" Fliss suddenly whispered. She

shone her torch over to the far corner of the building.

There on the ground was a tiny bat. The man went over and very gently picked it up. You ought to have seen it. It was so tiny, and its wings looked far too big for it somehow.

"I think it's probably just hungry," the man said. "We'll take it back with us and have it checked over. My guess is that it'll just need feeding up. Then we can release it back here in a day or two. Would you like to hold it?"

Oh, man! I don't know why people think bats are so scary, they're just gorgeous, all soft and cute. It looked a weeny bit like my rat Merlin, only it was a lot smaller – and it had wings of course!

I thought that Fliss would rather have her hair chopped off than hold a bat, but I was wrong. After a little persuasion she held her hand out – and was totally smitten.

"Isn't it just so *cute*!" she kept squeaking. "You're just adorable aren't you, little batty!"

The poor guy had to virtually prise it off her so that he could put it in his special bat box.

"Ah, here you are!" Dad suddenly appeared. "Seeing all the bats really takes me back to my childhood, Bob. I remember coming here for the holidays and being absolutely fascinated by them."

"Dad! You *knew* about the bats and you didn't say anything?" I accused him.

"Sorry Kenny, I didn't think," he shrugged. "Anyway you lot, it's supper time. Come on then, look lively!"

I don't think any of us really wanted to tear ourselves away from the bats, but it was getting kind of chilly.

"How will we find out if the bat's all right?" I asked.

"Well, you can ask Gordon here tomorrow night." Uncle Bob slapped the chief bat-watching guy on the shoulder. "All my batty friends will be coming to the party!"

"Excellent!"

As we were saying our goodbyes, the woman asked, "How come you thought we were vampires?"

Hmm, good question.

"Well, we'd seen shapes when we explored

round the chapel earlier in the week," I began.

"And saw the torches and heard noises," Rosie continued.

"Then when we came back there were all these footprints," Frankie added.

"And we found this cross." Lyndz rummaged in her pocket. "So we thought, you know, someone was trying to fend off a vampire or something."

"My cross!" The woman's face lit up. "I knew I'd lost it here the other night but I never thought I'd find it again! This is brilliant!"

Lyndz handed the cross over.

"I'm Shelley by the way," she said. "It's been great meeting you guys. I'll bring some information on bats to the party if you like. There are probably some roosting near where you live. You could form a bat group of your own!"

"Cool!"

"Excellent idea!"

"Well, that was an unexpected way to spend the evening!" Frankie mused as we walked back to the house. "I'm kind of glad we didn't have to fight off any vampires though, aren't you Kenz?"

"Nah, I was well up for it. Ha-yah!" I launched into a manic kickboxing frenzy.

"That's not what it looked like to us," spluttered Fliss. "It looked like you were peeing your pants when that guy grabbed you!"

"Oh yeah!" I stopped and stood in front of them menacingly. "We'll see who pees their pants when we've got to eat that haggis at the party tomorrow!"

And with that rather gruesome thought we all ran screaming into the house!

CHAPTER TEN

Now, as you know, I am Kenny 'Party Animal' McKenzie, so I was well up for Uncle Bob's little shindig – especially as the house was trimmed up like you wouldn't believe. Besides the balloons and stuff we'd put up, Lyndz's parents had really gone to town with the decorations. They're both dead artistic. In fact Lyndz's dad is the Head of Art and Design at the Comprehensive back in Cuddington.

Uncle Bob produced tons of spare tartan material (don't ask why he had it, I don't know). As soon as Lyndz's mum saw it, her eyes lit up.

"This is marvellous, Bob!" she squealed. "We could decorate your home like it's never been decorated before. Hey Keith!" she called out to Lyndz's dad. "Come here and take a look at this!"

We all looked at each other and shrugged. I mean, maybe it's an adult thing, but I couldn't see what was so exciting about a bit of checked cloth! Anyway, Mr and Mrs Collins sat huddled over the table for ages, making loads of drawings. Then they set to work on the dining room and the lounge. They swathed tartan around the walls and draped it over the tables. It looked just amazing. And all the time they were doing it they were giggling like teenagers and sneaking the occasional kiss when they thought we weren't looking – gross! Poor Lyndz was so embarrassed she couldn't watch.

"Well, I think it's cool!" Fliss told her. "I mean, it's much better than your mum being miserable like she was before, isn't it?"

"Yeah, I guess!" Lyndz admitted.

The Sleepover Club did our bit with the

decorations for the party too. We made all these bat shapes and hung them up in the hall so they looked as though they were flying about.

"Great bats, girls!" Uncle Bob looked at them admiringly. "Or should that be 'vampires', eh Kenny?"

He started chuckling in that throaty way of his.

"Now girls," he continued. "I hope you won't be too tired by this evening. The dancing gets pretty wild in these parts, you know."

"That's just what we like!" I grinned, and we showed him just how wildly we can dance. Uncle Bob just stared at us with his mouth open. I guess it was a pretty scary sight.

"Do you want to borrow some of our tapes?" asked Frankie. "We've got all the top tunes: S Club 7, Hear' Say…"

"Well, that's very kind of you," he smiled, "but I have a band lined up. In fact I was just coming to welcome them. I saw their van coming up the driveway a minute ago."

"Excellent!"

"Who do you think it'll be?" asked Fliss excitedly. "What about Travis, they're Scottish aren't they? Or Texas?"

A *real band*! This was going to be amazing.

"Who are they? It can't be..." Frankie's voice trailed away as a group of elderly men were greeted warmly by Uncle Bob. They had various instruments with them – a couple of violins, an accordion, a flute, a huge drum kit and...

"Bagpipes?" we all gasped in horror.

"How can you possibly dance to bagpipes?" groaned Fliss.

And I have to admit that just at that moment, Uncle Bob's party sounded about as exciting as an evening of back-to-back news programmes on the telly.

"Look, we'll just have to make the best of it!" Lyndz said brightly when we were back in our room getting changed. "Everybody's gone to a lot of trouble for this party. And besides, it was great of your Uncle Bob to invite us up here in the first place. What would he think if we turned out to be a right load of moaning minnies, just because he's not having the music *we* like to dance to?"

Trust Lyndz to make us all see sense. And actually, we were way off-beam about the party anyway.

As soon as we got downstairs and mingled with the other guests, we started having a great time. Although we were just the *teensiest* bit under-dressed. All the men (including my dad and Lyndz's dad) were wearing kilts, and the women were wearing posh swirly tartan skirts.

"I told you we should have brought our best party clothes," Fliss hissed.

But Lyndz's mum came to the rescue when she provided us all with tartan sashes. At least when we put them on we didn't feel so left out (even though mine did clash with my football shirt!).

We'd been downstairs for a while when Shelley rushed up to us.

"I've been looking for you everywhere," she smiled. "I thought you might like these."

She gave each of us a bat badge and a great big information pack from the Bat

Conservation Trust. It looked really great, with special sections for people our age and everything.

"We'll definitely contact them," I promised.

"How's that little bat you took away?" Fliss asked her anxiously.

"Oh just fine!" Shelley reassured us. "Gordon was right, the poor wee mite needed feeding up. We'll probably bring him back tomorrow."

"Great!"

Suddenly a loud gong rang out from the hall.

"Ladies and gentlemen!" Uncle Bob announced very grandly. "Supper is served!"

Excitedly we followed everyone else through to the dining room and found our places. We were sitting with the bat watchers, which was pretty cool. Gordon, who had seemed such a misery-guts the previous evening, actually turned out to be a real laugh. He never stopped teasing us about being a vampire. He'd even brought some of those fangs you get from joke shops, and kept swooping over us pretending to bite our necks! In fact he was just pretending to ravage Fliss when the most appalling racket filled the air.

"Sounds like Headless Eric has met with another victim!" I whispered to Frankie.

"Don't be daft!" she chided. "It's the bagpipes!"

You'll never believe what happened next. It was awesome. First the piper came into the room playing his pipes, followed by Mrs Barber who was carrying – *the haggis*! Bizarre or what? Then it got even stranger when Uncle Bob started reciting "Ode to a Haggis" by some guy called Robbie Burns.

"Do they normally talk to their food like that?" Fliss asked, looking bewildered.

Actually we didn't understand a word of the poem, but everyone else seemed to know it by heart. But the absolute best bit was at the end when Uncle Bob got out this silver dagger and stabbed the haggis so that the steam burst out of it and its smell filled the dining room. It didn't smell too bad actually, but Frankie went quite green just thinking about what was in it. Now you know me, I usually try anything once, but I was with Frankie on this one. We just looked on politely as everyone else tucked in and washed it all down with 'wee drams' of whisky. (If you ask me, the whisky smelt worse than the haggis!)

"Now I didn'ae want to confuse anyone," Uncle Bob stood up, grinning. "This isn'ae January the twenty-fifth, so we're not celebrating Burns Night again. I just thought no-one would object to sharing all the pageant of one of our greatest celebrations with our wee Sassenach friends."

A loud cheer went up.

"But don't you bairns fret," he continued. "You're not going to go hungry. Bring out the feast, Mrs Barber!"

And what a feast it was! It was all authentic Scottish grub too. We had Scottish beef (well, Frankie didn't obviously) and mashed 'neeps and tatties' (mashed turnips and potatoes to you and me). And for pudding there was 'clootie dumpling'. I know it sounds weird but it was a fruity pudding. Gordon told us that it got its name from the 'cloot' or cloth it's wrapped in whilst it's cooking!

After we'd finished eating, one of Uncle Bob's cronies, Angus, stood up and recited another poem.

"Crikey! Are they going to go on like this all night?" Rosie wondered.

I know it sounds dead boring listening to poetry, but it wasn't at all. At least Angus's one was easier to understand. It was about this guy, Lochinvar, who ran off with someone else's bride or something. It was a bit gushy but Fliss loved it.

"Right everyone!" Uncle Bob announced at the end of the recitation. "Let the dancing commence!"

Cheering, everyone made their way into the lounge where the band was warming up.

Now, I don't know if you remember my efforts at line dancing when we had our Fun Day at Mrs McAllister's stables? Well, my attempts at Scottish country dancing were even worse than that! It was just so confusing! There were Scottish reels and jigs and dancing in squares. We 'Stripped the

Willow', performed 'A Highland Welcome' and danced something called, believe it or not, 'The Elephant Walk'! It was great fun and nobody bothered at all when we messed up. Poor Gordon though, I trod on his toes so many times he eventually announced that he was "retiring injured".

We danced for so long that I thought my legs were going to drop off.

"This is more exhausting than a soccer match!" I gasped, collapsing into a chair.

"You're not kidding!" agreed Frankie, flopping next to me. "I'm completely wrecked."

"Hey girls, have you any idea what time it is?" Mum was being swung wildly around the dance floor by Uncle Bob. She was kind of pink in the cheeks, but she looked as though she was enjoying herself.

"Yeah guys, it's almost midnight!" Dad came over to us. "We've a long drive ahead of us tomorrow and I want to make an early start. I'll be calling it a night myself soon."

I certainly was very tired.

"Are Molly and Carli going to bed too?" I asked.

"They've been in bed *ages!*" Dad laughed.

"Losers!" I grinned. "They just couldn't stand the pace, could they?"

We said goodnight to everyone and promised to keep in touch with Shelley. As we went upstairs Lyndz's mum and dad were spinning round together in the centre of a circle whilst everyone else clapped.

"What are they like?" Lyndz groaned. But you could tell that she was really chuffed that they both looked so happy.

We crashed out as soon as we got into bed. No midnight feast, nothing.

It was a huge shock to the system, having to get up early the next day. Not only that, but as soon as we'd had breakfast Dad was eager to be off.

"Thank you so much, Uncle Bob!" We all hugged him, before we piled into Lyndz's van. "We've had the best time ever!"

"Well, you're welcome to come back whenever you want!" he grinned warmly. "I can't guarantee you any vampires, but we have ghosts a-plenty in these parts!"

As we were driving off, Fliss said, "Do you

think there really *are* ghosts here? He seemed pretty serious, didn't he?"

"I don't know about ghosts, Fliss," Lyndz's mum piped up from the front. "But there's certainly magic in the air at Bob's place."

Lyndz's father smiled at her and she leaned over and stroked his cheek.

"Yukarama!" Lyndz moaned, and we all burst out laughing.

"You know, we never did ask Molly whether it was her and Carli who pretended to be Headless Eric that night," Frankie mused.

"That's right! We'll ask the slimy snake as soon as we stop," I promised.

And that's exactly what we did. But you know what? She just went very white and stuttered:

"W-we thought it was you!"

"What? That second time, when Mum turned on the lights?" I asked.

"Yeah. Mum told us that she thought you'd been having a laugh the night before. So when we heard the noises again we were coming to sort you out!" Molly explained. We could see by her face that she was dead serious.

"So if it wasn't you," Fliss squealed, "who was it?"

Now I don't know about you, but I have serious doubts about the whole thing. Part of me thinks that maybe it was Uncle Bob having a laugh. You've seen what a barmy old goat he can be. But part of me really believes it *was* Headless Eric spooking us out in the attic. I reckon we'll have to go back up to Scotland soon, to do some serious *ghost-busting* this time. What do you think?

IF YOU ARE INTERESTED IN BATS
CONTACT:

The Bat Conservation Trust
15 Cloisters House
8 Battersea Park Road
London
SW18 4BG

or check out their website at:
www.bats.org.uk